Dedicated to Eric Dekker who helped me do this new version of this book • Remy Charlip
Text copyright © 1966, 1994, 2001 by Remy Charlip and Burton Supree • Pictures copyright © 1966, 1994, 2001 by Remy Charlip
All rights reserved • Originally published by Parents' Magazine Press, 1966 • First Tricycle Press printing, 2001
Library of Congress Catalog Card Number 00-010696 • ISBN-13: 978-1-58246-043-7 / ISBN-10: 1-58246-043-4

Has anybody seen my hat?

Tricycle Press • P.O. Box 7123 • Berkeley, California • 94707 • www.tricyclepress.c
Printed in Singapore • 4 5 6 7 8 — 10 09 08 07 06

MOTHER MOTHER I FEEL SICK
SEND FOR THE DOCTOR
QUICK
QUICK
QUICK

REMY CHARLIP & BURTON SUPREE
WITH PICTURES BY REMY CHARLIP

TRICYCLE PRESS • BERKELEY • TORONTO

I'll come right over. Don't you worry.

I've got lotions and potions
and powders and pills.
I've got all kinds of tonics for
all kinds of ills.

Whether itches or sneezes
or twitches or wheezes
or lumps or the mumps
or one single pimple...   I'll cure it! It's simple!

Look at him now, he's all green in the face!

I've never seen such a terrible case.

Let's rush him to the hospital this very minute.

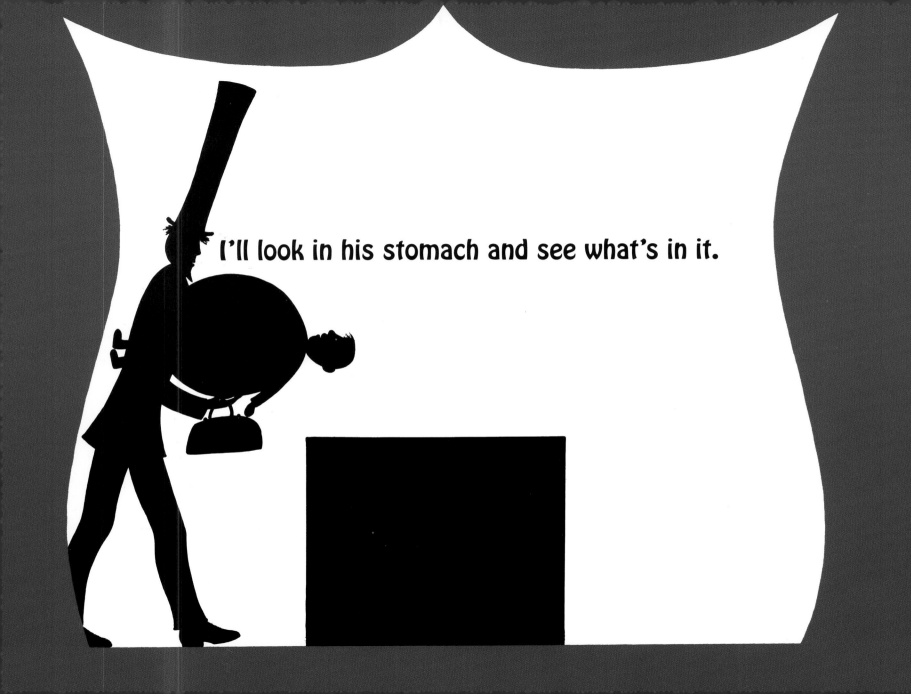

Did one green apple cause the trouble
and swell his stomach more than double?

One! Two! Three! And one's a ball!

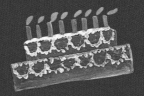

He ate a whole big birthday cake.

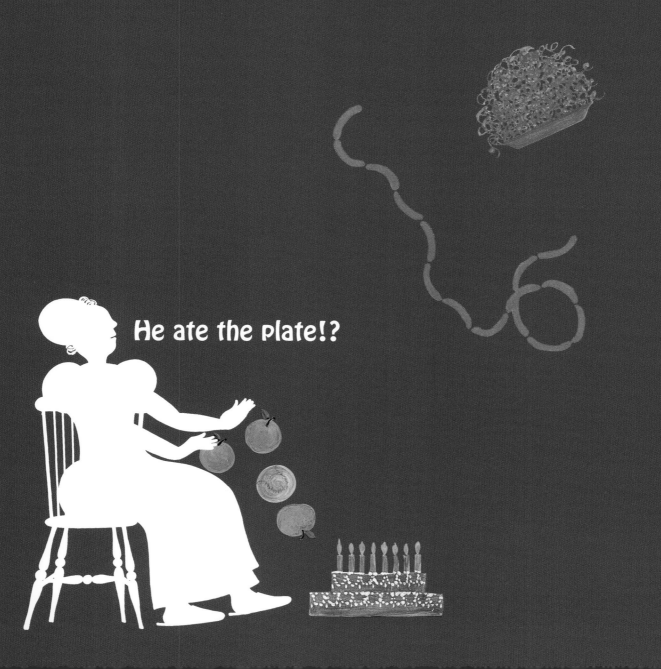

That's a rabbit!
And there's my hat!
I knew I didn't lose that hat.

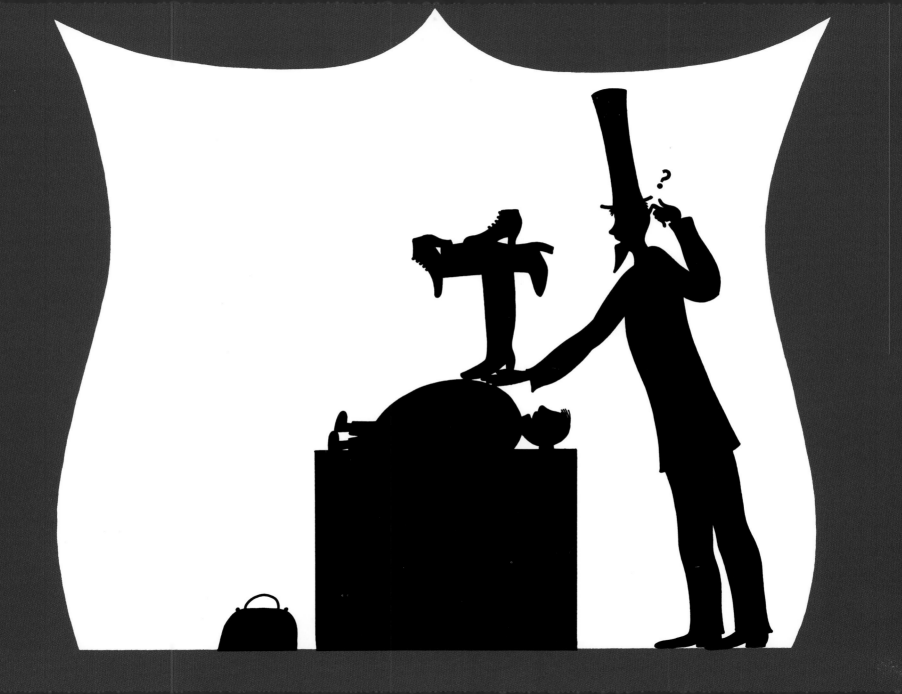

And there are my galoshes and shoes!
I didn't notice they were gone.
I even thought I had them on.

I think we're coming to the end.

Fly down here, my long lost friend.

Now don't catch cold.
Button up your sweater.

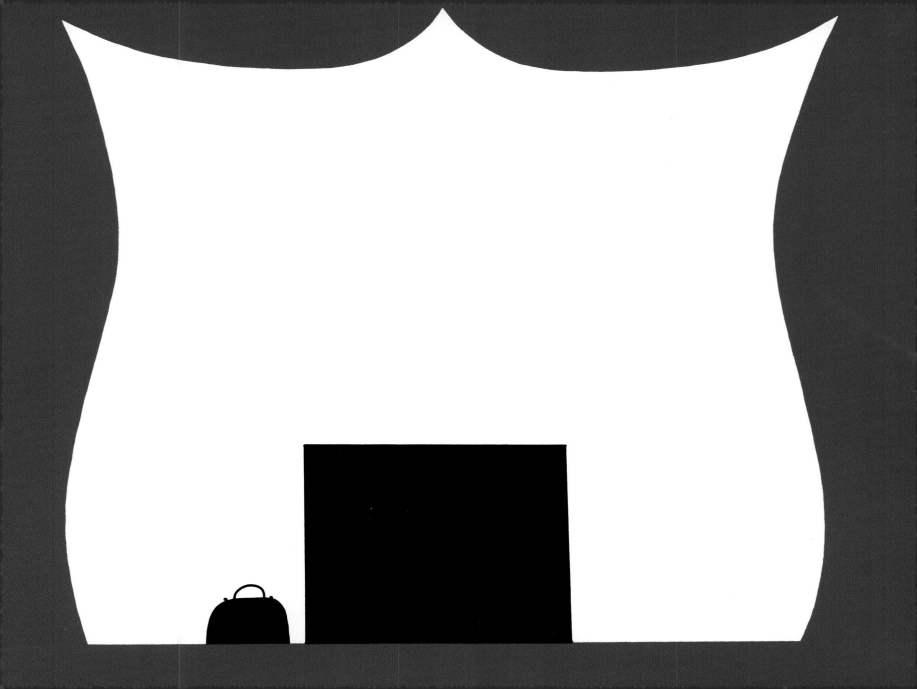

You can do this story as a shadow play for friends and family. It's simple. Just hang up a sheet behind which a child lies on a table. The doctor, with much oohing and aahing, pulls out each object or cardboard cut-out from a box below. A strong lamp from behind the sheet projects the shadows of the players and each object, to the delight of the audience.